How to Draw

FASHION FLATS

For Kids

Author Tony R. Smith

Example #1 Practice

Example of (Smudge Shading). Smudge Shading will give your drawing a complete look.

Example of (Tonal Shading). Tonal Shading will give your drawing a smooth contrast finish.

Example of (Light Smudge Shading). Light Smudge Shading will give your drawing a complete look.

Example of (Hatching Shading). Hatching Shading will help blend your drawing together.

Example #1 Final Drawing

Draw/Sketch

Draw/Sketch

Draw/Sketch

Draw/Sketch

Draw/Sketch

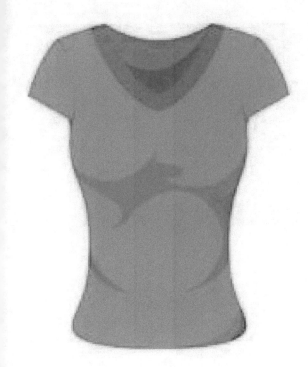
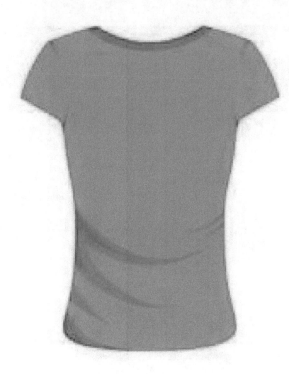

Draw/Sketch

Draw/Sketch

Draw/Sketch

Draw/Sketch

Fashion

Draw/Sketch

Draw/Sketch

Draw/Sketch

Draw/Sketch

Draw/Sketch

Draw/Sketch

Draw/Sketch

Draw/Sketch

Draw/Sketch

Draw/Sketch

Draw/Sketch

Draw/Sketch

Draw/Sketch

Draw/Sketch

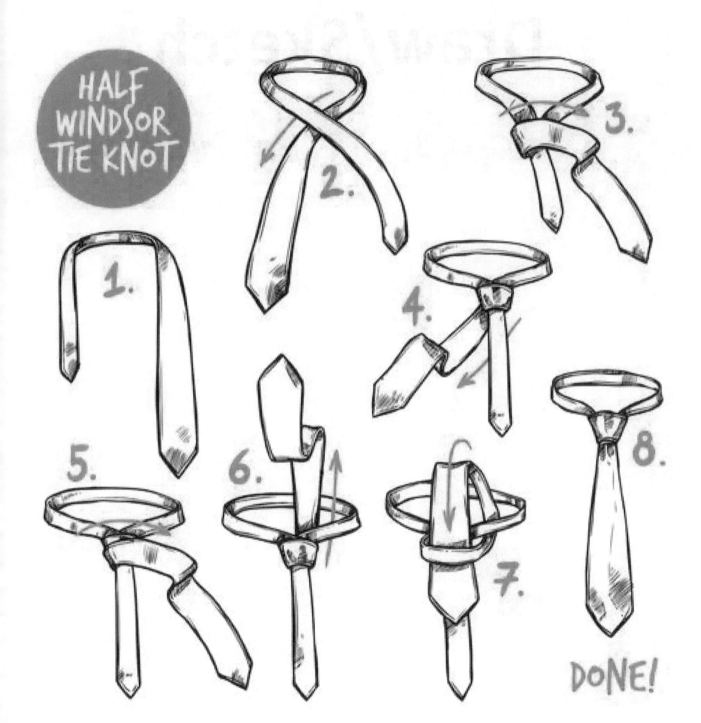

HALF
WINDSOR
TIE KNOT

1.

2.

3.

4.

5.

6.

7.

8.

DONE!

Draw/Sketch

Draw/Sketch

Draw/Sketch

Draw/Sketch

Draw/Sketch

Draw/Sketch

Draw/Sketch

Draw/Sketch

Draw/Sketch

Draw/Sketch

Draw/Sketch

Draw/Sketch

Draw/Sketch

Draw/Sketch

Draw/Sketch

Draw/Sketch

Draw/Sketch

Draw/Sketch

Draw/Sketch

Draw/Sketch

Draw/Sketch

Draw/Sketch

Draw/Sketch

Draw/Sketch

Draw/Sketch

Draw/Sketch

Draw/Sketch

Draw/Sketch

Draw/Sketch

Draw/Sketch

Draw/Sketch

Made in United States
Troutdale, OR
11/27/2023